I0648896

Charles Kerry

**A History of Waverly Abbey, in the County of Surrey**

Charles Kerry

**A History of Waverly Abbey, in the County of Surrey**

ISBN/EAN: 9783337326203

Printed in Europe, USA, Canada, Australia, Japan

Cover: Foto ©Andreas Hilbeck / pixelio.de

More available books at **www.hansebooks.com**

A

# HISTORY

OF

# 𝕸𝖆𝖛𝖊𝖗𝖑𝖊𝖞 𝕬𝖇𝖇𝖊𝖞,

IN THE

## COUNTY OF SURREY,

BY

## REV. CHARLES KERRY,

CURATE OF PUTTENHAM.

---

GUILDFORD:

PRINTED AND PUBLISHED BY ANDREWS AND SON, HIGH STREET.

1872.

TO

THOMAS D. ANDERSON, ESQ.,

OF

WAVERLEY ABBEY,

THIS ACCOUNT OF THE FIRST CISTERCIAN CONVENT

ESTABLISHED IN ENGLAND

is most respectfully dedicated

BY

THE AUTHOR.

# Preface.

THIS little Book contains the substance of a Lecture delivered at Puttenham, and subsequently, by request at Farnham, on Shrove Tuesday, 1872.

A few additions have been made, which probably would not have been of much interest to a general audience, but which will be valued by the Antiquarian and Topographer.

The extracts from the " Annals of Waverley " have been carefully translated from the edition published by the Record Commission, and it is believed that nothing has been omitted relative to the History of Waverley itself.    The other authorities which have been consulted are—

Documents preserved at the Record Office and British Museum, Histories of Surrey by Manning and Bray, and Brayley.

Papers and correspondence in the possession of Mr. Anderson, the present owner of the estate.

Dugdale's Monasticon.

Leland's Collections by Hearne, William of Malmsbury, and Rymer's Fœdera.

The Treatise has been published at the special request of Mr. Anderson, whose kindness in this undertaking, the Writer begs most heartily to acknowledge,

CHARLES   KERRY.

# Waverley.

MORE have heard of the Waverley Novels than have heard of Waverley and its Abbey, and many, perhaps, who know Waverley, and have seen the ruins of the old Cistercian Convent there, have wondered whether there is any connection between the title of the celebrated Novels and the name of the place itself. It seems that there is a link :—

" I recollect hearing (writes Leonard Norries, Esq., to 'the late owner of Waverley) that Sir Walter Scott—being engaged in some researches in the State Paper Office, or Record Office, I know not which—came by accident upon some documents relating to the Abbey, that stands in your park, and that these documents suggested the name to him.

The word "Waverley"* probably signifies the "Water-meadow ;" a very appropriate name, since the valley seems to have been subject to frequent inundations.

---

* Wa, We, or Wœ indicating *water*, is common to Wave, Wet, Weather, Well, &c. It is also found in the names of rivers, Wandle, *Wey*, Waveney, Wansbeck, Wessel. Wady (river ; Arab :) Wawa (N. Amer.) The primary radical appears in Ouse, Usk, Whiskey, from the celtic "Wysg," a current or stream, the very foam of the waters being " Ysgai." If *W* be taken for " *oo*," this will give the key to the inundations. Comp also *Avon*, &c.

# Foundation of the Abbey.

—

**W**AVERLEY Abbey was founded by William Giffard.*
Bishop of Winchester, on Christmas-day, in the year
1128. The monks, twelve in number, came with John,
their Abbot, from the Cistercian Convent of D'Aumone, in Nor-
mandy, an offshoot of the great Abbey of Cisteaux, from whence the
Cistercian order derived its name.

---

* Of the amiable character of William Giffard, the founder of Waverley Abbey, the
annals of Winchester afford the most charming testimony.  There was, perhaps, no
monastery in England which contained, at that time, a more fractious and insubor-
dinate fraternity than the Benedictine Abbey of Winchester.  Its inmates were an
endless source of trouble and annoyance to their Bishop.  Nevertheless, we are told
that after all his trials with them, " as though his heart loved each and all of them,"
whenever he came to Winchester, his first visit was to them.

On his entrance into their church, he would at once kneel down and pray for them,
and when with tears he had cause to visit them, he always associated with them
both in the cloister and refectory, and never left them without his blessing.

As often as he could, he sought occasion to be with them both in the dormitory
and in the refectory, where, very frequently, he sat in the lowest place among the
novices, so that all might be benefitted by his bright example.  At length, having
been received as a monk in the infirmary of the monks, he there surrendered his
spirit to God in the year 1128—the very winter in which he founded Waverley.

# The Cistercians.

THE origin of the Cistercians is thus related by William of Malmsbury, who lived about the year 1140, that is to say, only twelve years after Waverley was founded.

" The Cistercian Order is now both believed and asserted to be the surest road to heaven.—It redounds to the glory of England to have produced the distinguished man who was the author and pro-moter of that Rule. To us he belonged, and in our schools passed the earlier part of his life. He was named Harding, and born in England of no very illustrations parents. From his early years he was a monk at Sherbourne, but when secular desires had captivated his youth, he grew disgusted with the monastic garb, and went first to Scotland, and afterwards to France. Here he become awakened to the love of God. He went, soon afterwards, to Rome, with a clerk, who shared his studies; but no obstacles on the way, neither its length, nor their poverty, prevented them from singing the whole Psalter daily, both as they went and returned.

" Returning into Burgundy, he was shorn at Molesmes—a new and magnificent monastery. Here he soon learnt the deviations of monastic life from the primitive rule. The Abbot and eighteen monks, among whom was Stephen, left that Abbey, declaring that the purity of the institution could not be preserved in a place where riches and gluttony warred against even the heart that was well inclined. They, therefore, retired to Cisteaux, and there founded the first house of the Cistercian Order."

Malmsbury, after this, proceeds to give an account of the Cistercian Rule—the Rule of the monks of Waverley.

# Rule.

"CERTAINLY," says Malmsbury, "many of their regulations seem severe, and more particularly these :—

"They wear nothing made of furs or linen, nor even that finely-spun linen garment, which we call 'Staminium' a kind of woollen shirt); neither breeches, unless when sent on a journey, which, at their return, they wash and restore.

"They have two tunics with cowls, but no additional garment in winter, though, if they think fit, in summer they may lighten their garb.

"They sleep clad and girded, and never, after matins, return to their beds; but they so order the time of matins, that is shall be light ere the lauds begin. So intent are they on their Rule, that they think no jot or tittle of it should be disregarded.

" Directly after these hymns, they sing the prime, after which, they go out to work for stated hours. They complete whatever labour or service they have to perform by day, without any other light.

" No one is ever absent from the daily services, or from compline, except the sick.

" The cellarer and hospitaller, after compline, wait upon the guests, yet observing the strictest silence.

" The Abbot allows himself of no indulgence beyond the others— everywhere present—everywhere attending to his flock; except that he does not eat with the rest, because his table is with the strangers and poor. Nevertheless, be he where he may, he is equally sparing of food and of speech; for never more than two dishes are served either to him or to his company. Lard and meat never, but to the sick.

" From the Ides (13th) of September till Easter, they do not take more than one meal a day, except on Sunday. They never leave the cloisters but for the purpose of labour, nor do they ever speak either there or elsewhere, save only to the abbot or prior."

They pay unwearied attention to the canonical services, making

no addition to them, except the vigil for the defunct. They use in
their divine service, the Ambrosian chants and hymns, as far as
they were able to learn them at Milan.

While they bestow care on the stranger and the sick, they inflict
intolerable mortifications on their own bodies for the health of their
souls.*

After a long account of them, Malmsbury thus makes his summary :—"But to comprise briefly all things which are or can be
said of them—the Cistercian monks of the present day, are a model
for all monks, a mirror for the diligent, a spur to the indolent."

As to the discipline and moral status of Waverley Abbey in the
days of its prosperity, (and those are always the times of the
greatest danger) the following calculation will afford the most satis-
factory testimony :—

In 163 years, viz.—from the foundation of the Abbey to 1291,
when the Annals of Waverley end, no less than seven of the monks
of Waverley were elected to be Abbots of their own house, and
four more of them chosen to be the heads of other religious estab-
lishments.   Now, if we find so many promotions in 163 years, how
many more must there have been during the remaining 245 years,
of which we have but little, or no record ?

* There is a notice in the Annals of Waverley about some alteration in the Rule.
Anno 1257, " It was appointed in this year, by a general chapter, that for the future
there should be twelve shavings of the tonsure during the year, where previously
there were but seven.   And that at the altar the Abbots should use copes, and the
attendant ministers, dalmatics, as is contained in the uses."

# Abbey Buildings.

THE following portions of the Abbey are mentioned in original records relating to Waverley : the CHURCH, with its tower and transept ; the CHAPTER-HOUSE ; the TREASURY; the INFIRMARY of the SECULARS ; the INFIRMARY ; the CHAPEL of the INFIRMARY; the REFECTORY, the GUEST-HOUSE, with its CHAMBERS ; the LAVATORY; the GATEWAY by the river; the CHAPEL of S. MARY at the Convent Gate; the FOUR STONE BRIDGES.

Monastic edifices, and especially those belonging to the Cistercian Order, were, for the most part, erected on the same general plan, the buildings being arranged so as to enclose a court or quadrangle, around which was constructed a covered walk or cloister, which not only connected the various offices of the establishment, but also formed a convenient ambulatory for the inmates in wet weather.

On the north side of this court the Church was almost invariably erected, and very wisely, because it afforded an agreeable shelter from the northerly winds.

On the eastern side, stretching southwards, came the Sacristry, (usually adjoining the south transept) the Chapter-house, with Song-school, Library and Scriptorium, adjacent, often occupying an upper story ; here too, was usually situated the Treasury, while further to the south, stood the Common-room of the monks, generally at the south-east angle of the cloister-square.

On the south side contiguous to the Abbey stream, stood the Refectory or Dining-hall, the Kitchen, the " Garderobe," and other offices, the refuse of which was swept away by the river. At Fountains Abbey, York, the kitchen was cooled, when necessary, by the admission of a current of air through a trap from the culvert beneath.

The buildings on the west side of the quadrangle were usually devoted to the lodging and entertainment of strangers. Here stood the " Guest-hall " at Waverley, with its " Chambers," probably extending from the present fragment near the river, with its fine vaulting and marble columns, to the south-west corner of the church, a distance little less than a hundred yards.

The centre of the cloister-square was occupied by the Lavatory.

# The Abbey Church of S. Mary.

NOT a fragment of the original Norman Church of William Giffard (the founder) remains. It appears to have yielded gradually to the new structure, commenced in 1203. This was a cruciform edifice, and consisted of choir, transepts, and nave, with a tower rising at the intersection. There appears to have been three chapels in each of the transepts, as well as others at the east end of the choir. The extreme length of the church was 322 feet; breadth of nave and choir, (including aisles,) 73 feet; and the extreme width at the transepts, 163 feet.

This new and magnificent structure was commenced under the devoted auspices and supervision of William, Rector of the Church of Bradewater, on the 18th day of April, 1203. No sooner, however, were the foundations dug, and busy hands had begun to rear the structure, than the poor monks of Waverley were arrested by a grievous famine, and they, who were ever ready to feed and shelter the destitute, were compelled to seek an asylum in other religious homes. "Anno 1203. There was a great famine, and dying of men. In this year the monks of Waverley were scattered through divers houses (cells or monasteries) by reason of the very great scarcity of produce."—(Annals)  Nor was this the only hindrance : it appears from the Close Rolls, anno 1208, that as soon as this kingdom was placed under an interdict by the Pope, King John laid hands on the property of all ecclesiastics, the possessions of William of Bradewater amongst the rest.  "The King to Adam Tysum and Adam Esturmy, &c.  We command you that ye permit William, Priest of Bradewater, who, out of his goods, made work at the church of Waverley, to have and to hold, in quiet possession, all his tenements in our Bailliwick (taken into our hands by reason of the interdict) to carry on the work aforesaid."  (Rot : Lit : Claus : Anno 9. John. Memb. 4.)

Hence we learn that the Abbey Church of Waverley was re-built at the expense of this good and self-denying man.

The Church was so far completed in the year 1214, that then five altars were dedicated.  There can be no doubt but that the east end of the Church was finished first, and that the numerous altars occupied the chapels at the end of the choir.  Here is the full account from the Annals :  "Anno 1214.  On the festival of the seven brothers, five altars were dedicated by Albin,* Lord Bishop of Ferns, of our Order, in the presence of Peter de Rupibus, Lord

---

* This Albin, surnamed O'Mulloy, Bishop of Ferns, in Ireland, succeeded Joseph O'Hethe in the See in 1185. He died, very old, about the end of the year 1222, having been Bishop about thirty-six years.—(Alban Butler.)

Bishop of Winchester. At the same time, he blessed the cemetery (or rather, perhaps, the graves) of those who had died whilst the Convent was under interdict, and he blessed all the crosses of the church, and annointed them with holy oil."

In the year 1218, a great bell was provided for the Convent, which seems to indicate the probable completion of the central tower about this time. "It was provided by the counsel and aid of Adam, the Lord Abbot of Waverley (1st of the name) 'for never until that time (says the annalist) had they more than one bell in the afore-said house.'" Four more years pass by, and the great bell tolls for the master builder. In 1222, William of Bradewater, closes his eyes on his cherished work for ever. We are not told into whose hands he resigned his plummet, or square, or what his last words of instructions were. Here is the simple record : "Anno 1222. William, rector of the Church of Broadwater, of pious memory, who began the new church of Waverley, died in the 20th year after the work was begun, and he is buried in the door-way (foris) or at the entrance near to (juxta) the south wall of the same church. On whose soul may He have mercy, who alone after death is able to apply the healing."—(Annals.)

Eight years after Bradewatere's departure, the transepts were completed. "Anno 1231. On the Festival of S. Barnabas, two altars were consecrated, one in the south cross of our Church, by

Lord John, then Bishop-Vicar for the Lord Bishop of Winchester.
On the day also of their consecration, he granted to the persons
adoring there, ten days of remission. The same Bishop granted
the same days of indulgence when he dedicated three altars in the
north transept."—(Annals.)

The choir, transepts, central tower, and western abutments were
now constructed.

Now comes the evidence as to the probable site of the old
Church. The old building was obviously in the way, and the new
nave was not yet finished. It may, therefore, be presumed that the
old Church was gradually removed to make way for the new one.

" Anno 1231. The Monks of Waverley entered the new Church
from the first old Church with a solemn procession, and joy of great
devotion, on the Feast of S. Thomas the Apostle, in the 30th year
from the commencement of the new Church, whose founder
(inceptor) was William of Bradewatere, of happy memory."—
(Annals.)

" In the year 1236, Giffard, formerly Abbot of Bettlesdene, and
tenth Abbot of Waverley, succeeded Abbot Adam, who retired this
year from his Abbacy. This Giffard instituted a private mass to be
celebrated on the obits of those who had been yearly benefactors to
the Convent. He also appointed that on Xmas-day, and on the
Feast of All Saints, lighted candles should be provided for all the

altars which are in our Church, whilst the divine office is celebrated in it, viz.—to both vespers, and to nocturns, and to lauds, and to masses, which also our whole convent desire to be observed from henceforth."—(Annals.)

"Anno 1238. Peter de Rupibus, Bishop of Winchester, died in his castle at Farnham, whose heart* and bowels were interred in the Church of the Blessed Mary of Waverley, but his body was carried to Winchester, and there interred honorably in the Church of his See."—(Annals.)

This was the Bishop by whose instrumentality (in the year 1215) the Farnham market was transferred from the Sunday to the Thursday, on which day it has ever since been held.

"Anno 1239. In this year, in the time of Giffard, Lord Abbot, a larger bell was provided for our house, and it began to be first struck for the hours on Easter-day. Its name is to be found in these lines, which are written on the bell :—

> "Thy name I bear, O virgin spouse of Christ.
> His guardian wast thou, I proclaim thy praise."

* About the year 1700, the heart of Peter de Rupibus was unfortunately discovered by some *heartless* grubbers, and removed from its sacred resting-place. It was enclosed in a leaden box, containing a saline liquid; and when Manning and Bray wrote their History at the beginning of this century, it was in the possession of John Martyr, Barrister, of Guildford, whose father, the Town Clerk, had it from Mr. Child, a former owner of Waverley. One naturally asks, what has become of the leaden box with the heart of one of the best and ablest of the Bishops of Winchester? Perhaps, *unlabelled*, both box and heart have been thrown out into a ditch, by some ignorant executor, as so much rubbish; or, what is equally horrible, it may have been dealt out in small portions, and carried away in screws of paper by curiosity-seekers, or Protestant admirers of relicks.

The following incident is connected with the Church, and may
fitly be recorded here :—

" Anno 1245. On Palm Sunday, which this year fell on the 1st
of April, Aleanor, Countess of Leicester, (sister of King Henry 3rd)
a most sincere lover of our house, by favour of the Pope, was permitted to enter into our Abbey, having for her husband that most
worthy man, Simon de Montfort, Earl of Leicester. With her
were her two sons, Henry and Simon, and three handmaidens, at
whose entrance (into the Church) a remarkable circumstance hap-
pened, which is known to all. When she had placed her foot
within the door of the Church, exactly opposite the great altar
where the mass of the Blessed Virgin was then being celebrated by
the priest, the victim of salvation was being elevated at the time of
consecration, which we believe must be ascribed not to chance, but
to divine appointment, and that the love of Jesus led her there, that
that she might offer unto his most benign presence such things as
were required. She presented there a cloth, very precious, which
was to be placed on the altar on the days on which the relics there
were exposed. She was present afterwards at the sermon in the
Chapter, at the procession and at the greater mass, and having
kissed the wood of the Lord, retired from the Abbey greatly edified.
Afterwards, we received of her gift five-and-twenty marks, and
eighteen marks more for the fabric of the Church ; and by her aid
also we accomplished the purchase of 125 acres of land at Netham."

PART OF SOUTH TRANSEPT DOORWAY.          [Vide p. 18.

The following narrative makes us long for more of such inter-esting details :—

"Anno 1248. A certain young man, by an unfortunate slip, fell headlong to the ground from the stone parapet on the summit of the tower of our Church, nevertheless, without the fracture of a limb. There he lay for some time breathless, as was supposed, but a little while after he regained his spirit, and began to speak, and not long after that, feeling no pain, he recovered altogether."—(Annals.)

He must have broken his fall on some of the roofs which met at the tower.

Nothing is recorded after this in the Annals, respecting the Church, for twenty-one years.

In the year 1269, on the 2nd day of June, John Breton was con-secrated Bishop of Hereford at Waverley Abbey, by Nicholas,* Lord Bishop of Winchester, assisted by Goffred* of Worcester, Richard* of S. Davids, William* of Llandaff, Walter of Salisbury, William* of Bath, Walter of Exeter,* and Roger,* Bishop of Lich-field and Coventry. The scene must have been most imposing, no less than eight Bishops took part in the ceremony.

It is an interesting fact, that the present clergy of the Church of England derive their Orders through no less than seven of the above named Bishops ; those marked with an asterisk () having assisted at the consecration of Robert Kilwardby, Archbishop of Canterbury, 26th February, 1273, at Canterbury. (Cron : Maj : 157. Wikes 99. Cont. Gervas MS. Polistoire MS. M : Westminst. vid. F. G. Lee's Validity of Eng. Orders, &c., &c.)

In the year 1274, a religious ceremony took place at Waverley, and unquestionably in the Abbey Church, which was considered worthy of remembrance in the Annals :—

"This year, in "Cœna Domini," (Maunday Thursday) the holy chrism was made (" confectum ") at Waverley, by that venerable màn, Nicholas, Bishop of Winchester, who, the same day, took food with the convent in the Refectory."

" Anno 1278. On the feast of S. Matthew, Apostle and Evange- list, the Church of Waverley was dedicated in honour of the glorious Virgin Mary, mother of God, by Nicholas de Hely, Lord Bishop of Winchester, who, to all present with pious devotion, granted one year's remission, and forty days of pardon to all who should frequent that place on the anniversary of its dedication for ever. The said Bishop, out of the abundance of his favour and devotion, being de- sirous that every thing relating to the said dedication should be accomplished with happiness and joy, magnificently supplied, at his own expense, on that day, provisions for all persons present."

So far the chronicle of Waverley. Wharton, in his Anglia Sacra, (vol. 1, p. 503) furnishes the following additional particulars from the Annals of Worcester :—

PART OF SOUTH TRANSEPT. [*Vide* p. 19.

" And not only on the first day, but even almost through the nine days solemnities, he sustained, with victuals, all who frequented the said place.

" No less than six abbots and other prelates were present on the occasion, very many knights and ladies, and so great a multitude of both sexes, that it was impossible to number them. The number of those who sat down to meat on the first day was 7066 of both sexes, and this was reckoned according to the distribution of dishes, and all these being refreshed by the overteeming generosity of the aforesaid Bishop, returned to their homes glorifying and praising God."

Another year and the earth of S. Mary's, Waverley, closes over him who had dedicated the fabric :—

" On the 1st of the Ides of February (i. e. 12th) Nicholas, Lord Bishop of Winchester, of happy memory, departed this life, and in the Church of the Blessed Mary of Waverley, which he had dedicated a little before, was committed to the tomb, with great devotion, by the venerable fathers, William, Bishop of Norwich, and Robert of Bath and Wells, and on the third day following, the heart of the said Bishop was interred in the cathedral church of Winchester by the same prelates."

Another interment, and then we have completed our account of S. Mary's :—

"Anno 1290. 9th Kal. of April, Lady Joane Ferre departed this life, and on the 7th Kalend of the same, which was then Palm Sunday, she was honourably interred in the Church of the Blessed Mary of Waverley before the altar of the Blessed Virgin aforesaid."[*]

But few architectural features of the Abbey Church remain, to so great an extent has the work of demolition been carried. The north wall of the nave aisle has a horizontal bead moulding, about six feet above the stone bench. This settle is visible on this side only, though probably it once extended round the building.

The base of the pier at the angle of the north aisle and the north transept also exists, though in a mutilated condition. There are three slender shafts with their tassel-like bases in the north wall, formerly supporting the groining of the north aisle, and with each of these are indications of a corresponding buttress outside. There must have been single lancets, similar to those in the south transept, in each of the spaces between these shafts. Each buttress has been about twelve feet apart. There were three buttresses on the western side of the north transept, and, consequently, three lancets corresponding with the three in the west wall of the south cross.

The door-way, leading into the cloister by the south transept, ex-

---

[*] Raymond de Ferre, in 1536, bore for arms, " gu. three plates within a bordure chequy arg and az."

WEST WALL OF SOUTH TRANSEPT AND CARROL. [Vide p. 19.

hibits the bases of the inner jamb mouldings in very fair preservation.

Some nice features are still to be seen in the south transept. The bases of the three west lancets, are in good preservation, and correspond with those in the Common Room overlooking the river. The south-east angle has a remarkable impost worthy of examination.

Nothing else remains to be noted, save the broken coffin of Purbeck marble lying immediately before the entrance to the choir.

The sun-dial, decorated with bats with outspread wings—significant of the desolation of the sanctuary—probably stands on the site of the high altar.

In the west wall of the south transept, within the cloister-square, is a remarkable recess, five feet deep and six feet wide, something like a blocked door-way. This, without doubt, was a "carrol," or small closet, fitted with shelves and lockers, to contain books for the use of scribes and studious monks. This arrangement is frequently mentioned in ancient writings,* and at Gloucester it is very apparent.

---

* The will of William Place, priest, proved in 1504, says—" Item. I bequeath to the monastery of Sergnt. Edmund, forseid, my book of the dowt of Holy Scrypture, to lye and remain in the cloister of the seid monastery, as long as it will there endure."—Vid. Brit. Arch. Assoc. Rep. vol. 21, p. 131.

# Chapter-House.

---

**A**DJOINING the south transept are the remains of what is
usually considered to have been the CHAPTER-HOUSE, of
which only the north and south walls remain. These, as
appears from without, are of Norman origin, being part of the work
of William Giffard, the founder, c. 1128. The builders of the south
transept, about a century afterwards, endeavoured to knit their
work to the more ancient wall of the Chapter-house, but as this
later wall has been partly destroyed, a Norman moulding has been
laid bare on the transept side. The south wall of the Chapter-
house has a blank Norman arcading on its southern exterior.

As the Chapter-house appears to have had an early English
vaulting, it must have been remodelled about the time the south
transept was constructed, when its character was changed from an
earlier to a later style.

The length of the Chapter-house is fifty feet, and its breadth
twenty-seven feet.

The Chapter-house was the place where the more important
affairs of the community were discussed and settled. In this room

delinquencies were tried, and punishment inflicted. After the chapter was ended, several monks usually stayed behind to confess their faults, and to receive discipline. The Chapter-house of Waverley occurs several times in the Annals.

"Anno 1194. William Maldut died six nones of October, and was buried before the door of the Chapter at Waverley." This name, in the margin of the printed copy, is termed "Manduit." If this be the correct form, he must have been allied to the Earls of Warwick, for in 1264, William Manduit, Earl of Warwick, was surprised by the adherents of Simon de Montford, (when holding Kenilworth) and the walls of Warwick Castle were then completely destroyed. (Arms—Argt. 2 bars gules).

"Anno 1225. Henry, King of England, was received in our house on the 17th day of January (16 Kal.) with a solemn procession. On the morrow, he entered the Chapter, and he desired and received the society, brotherhood, and participation of the benefits of our house."—(Annals.)

Here also in 1245, by express permission, the wife of Simon de Montfort, King Henry's sister, had the privilege of hearing a sermon, probably delivered by some distinguished member of the Convent.

"Anno 1262. William, Abbot of Ford (Co-Devon) died at Waverley, and was buried in the Chapter-house."

The south wall of the Chapter-house is continued eastwards be-

yond the line of the east end of the Abbey Church.   It may have
formed one of the walls of the Abbot's house, or a portion of the
Infirmary with its Chapel.   The latter suggestion is the more
feasible, because the burial ground of the Abbey was immediately
contiguous on the north and east, and because such an arrangement
would be exactly in accordance with the sentiments of those times.

Adjoining the Chapter-house, to the south, is a passage with a
semi-circular vaulting of stone.   This connected the cloister with
the premises on the east, the Infirmary, the Abbot's house, and
the Gardens of the Convent.   The door itself was fixed on the outer
side.   This passage formerly had bays in the vaulting, formed by
groins or ribs of a rectangular shape, resting on corbels inserted in
the impost mouldings at the sides.

In the vicinity of the Chapter-house, was usually situated

# The Treasury,

Of which there is mention in 1265.   In Croxden Abbey the
Treasury was on the upper story, adjoining the Church.   It is
obvious, from the following extract from the Annals, that the
Treasury at Waverley was not on the ground floor.

"Anno 1265.   In this year, on the 4th of the Kalends of December, viz.—on Saturday before the first Sunday in Advent, the water

of the river, overflowing its banks, ran into all the offices of the Abbey standing on the lower grounds, by reason of which, the Convent being troubled, some in the Church, some in the Treasury, some in the Chambers of the Guest-house, passed the following night as they were able, and for many days they were engaged in cleansing the houses."

The upper story of the Chapter-house usually formed the Scriptorium, or Writing-room, were the monks employed themselves in writing new books, or multiplying copies of old ones. The names of a few of the works, which adorned the monastic library at Waverley, are given by Leland, who lived at the time of the dissolution of monastic houses.

1.—Liber Heraclidis, ad Lausum.

2.—Sermones Odonis, Abbotis de Bello (liber desiderabatur)

3.—Eulogy of John Cornubiensis.

4.—An Epistle of Bede, concerning the Equinox.

5.—Book of Robert, Prior of S. Frideswide, concerning the marriage of James.

" Perchance," says Leland, " this writer is Robert of Crikeland, who collected the writings of Pliny, of which there is a copy at Hartland."

An odd assortment truly ! but unquestionably a most imperfect list, for that most valuable work, " The Annals," in not even named.

This work is still preserved in the British Museum. It is a small thick quarto of parchment, containing 197 leaves, of which the Annals occupy all but the first twenty-one. It has been written by several hands, and terminates, unfortunately, and somewhat abruptly, with the year 1291. We are indebted to monastic librarians for all the treasures of ancient English literature we possess. The more valuable of their works they transcribed with a care and a zeal most commendable, indeed their illuminated MSS. excite the wonder and astonishment of all who see them. Before the invention of printing, they multiplied copies of Holy Scripture, and through their means alone, the Word of God was circulated, though only the wealthy could afford to purchase the precious transcripts.

Continuing our course from the Church down the east side of the cloister, we come to

# The Common Room,

Of the monks, usually termed the Refectory—but the dining-room at Waverley has perished—it undoubtedly lay on the south, or water side of the quadrangle. This Common room is among the best preserved portions of the ruins. Its southern end, with its three lancet windows, is nearly entire, as well as its eastern and western walls. Both of these are pierced by two lancets, and the eastern wall, at its northern extremity, contains a small, low, square-headed window of

LANCET WINDOWS OF COMMON ROOM. [Vide p. 24.

the sixteenth century, probably inserted shortly before the dissolution in 1536. Two small niches have also been made in this wall within, as if for the insertion of an hour-glass, a candle, or some such thing. This room was probably constructed about the year 1230.

On the south side of the cloister were usually arranged the Refectory, or Dining-room, with the kitchen and its offices. A high blank wall, running parallel to the river, and almost connecting the Common-room with the Guest-hall, is all that remains of these buildings. There is a projection in it, almost midway, indicating the junction of a wall extending northwards towards the cloister, but nothing else that can be noticed, neither traces of chimney, doors, nor windows.

There is a notice of the Refectory, in 1274, when Nicholas de Hely, Bishop of Winchester, shared a meal with the Convent therein.

## The Guest-Hall.

HIS once beautiful structure probably extended from the river to the Church—a distance of about one hundred yards.

A small portion, near the river, with its single row of Purbeck-marble columns, and delicate groinings, is all that remains;

and would that this had remained intact.  About the year 1730, it
seems to have been converted into a summer-house, when its floor
was raised, and paved with large red tiles, concealing the bases of
the central columns, and a fire-place inserted in the place of the old
one.  At the same time, the windows, or at least, some of them,
appear to have been converted into doors, and other serious injuries
inflicted.  Enough, however, remains to testify to the original mag-
nificence of this part of the Abbey.

Here lodging and entertainment was provided for the visitors to
the Convent, and the numerous retainers who frequently accom-
panied the more distinguished guests.

The accommodation of the Guest-house must have been sorely
tested in the year 1208, when King John favoured Waverley with a
visit.  Fortunately he brought his wine with him,* or his thirsty
household would have fared but badly, for a little while before the
monks had been obliged to quit Waverley for lack of the necessaries
of life.  Although the King was no lover of ecclesiastics, this visit
seems to have made a favourable impression on the monarch, for
this year he returned the lands of William of Bradewater to their
owner, to enable him to carry on the building of the Abbey Church

---

* On 28 March, 1208, King John was at Pagham, (a port near Chichester).  On 6
April, 1208, the King (being at Guildford) allowed Ralph de Cornhill, £3 10s. 2½d., for
two tuns of wine (about 500 gallons) and for the carriage of them from Pagham to
Waverley, "for the consumption of our household there," during two days, viz.—
Maunday Thursday, and Good Friday, the 3rd and 4th of April, 1208.

INTERIOR OF GUEST CHAMBER. [*Vide p.* 25.

of Waverley. It is probable also, that about this time (if not during
this visit) the King made some grant to the Convent, for there was
a long suit in the time of Edward I. between the Abbot of Waverley
and William de Giselham, concerning twenty-four acres of land in
Essendon between Werdham and Wykes, which the Abbot declared
to have been given to the monks of Waverley by King John, but
which William de Giselham asserted were not included in the royal
grant.—(Placita de quo Warranto.)

With this royal visit must undoubtedly be associated THE
LIBERTIES OF WAVERLEY.

King John, by his charter, exempted the Convent from the
payment of taxes from Danegeld and Scutage; from payments
relating to murder and thefts; also concerning Hidage and
and Scotage of the shire and hundred; from payments relating to
levying of armies; from Pontage; from raising of castles, bridges,
and walls; from the formation of ponds and parks. They were to
be exempt concerning the payment of "Wardpeny," "Averpeny;"
pleas of plaintiffs; from Wapentake, and Leyrwyte, and Hengwyte,
and Flemenwyte, and Blodwyte, and Tenipeny; and concerning
Lastage and Stallage; and from all services and customs which
pertain to the king; and from all secular service, exaction, and
servile work. Freedom of court in all their boundaries was also
granted by the same charter.—(See Placita de quo Warranto Edwd.
I. Rot. 63d.)

QUERY.—Do these liberal grants and concessions afford any clue to the great consumption of wine at Waverley during the royal visit on 3rd and 4th of April, 1208 ?

It is very probable that the king's visit might have suggested the necessity for a more commodious Guest-hall, for the present one must have been erected shortly afterwards. Be this as it may, King John was in a very different humour in 1210, as appears from the Waverley Annals :—" But Waverley, with all her privileges withdrawn and taken away, her monks and lay brethren scattered round about through England, patiently sustained the wrath of the king. John III, Abbot of the same place, terrified by fear of the king, left his house, and fled away secretly in the night. These things were done about the feast of the B. Martin. The king also forbade that any of the Cistercian Order should cross the sea, or that any from foreign parts should come into England."

Above the Guest-hall were dormitories for the guests. The gable of this upper story still towers high above the water, casting its ivied reflection in the gentle stream. Two large windows, surmounted by an oriel, gave light through the gable, whilst the side walls of the dormitory were pierced with many narrow lights. Several of these were existing in 1735, as appears from an old print of that date.

In the centre of the cloister-square stood the

GUEST CHAMBER FROM RIVER. [*Vide p.* 25.

# Lavatory,

Of which indications were remaining in 1670, when Aubrey visited the Abbey.

"Anno 1179. At this time our Lavatory was constructed, and the Aqueduct provided."—(Annals.)

"Anno 1216. In this year, not without the surprise of many, the fountain of our Lavatory, called "Lude-welle," ceased to flow, and was almost dried up, whose productiveness, through the course of many years, had most copiously administered its waters to the divers offices in the Abbey. The spring, therefore, failing, and hardly flowing through the offices, serious inconvenience was doubtless experienced within the Abbey. This unfortunate circumstance, therefore, a certain monk of ours, brother Simon by name, considering and weighing gravely, began to ponder how the inconvenience might be remedied. Having sufficiently matured his plans, he girded himself bravely to the task of searching and digging for new veins of living waters; and these, after diligent search, he discovered, and with great labour and energy ("sudor") compelled them all to discharge their waters through undergrouud pipes into one place; and there he made by art a living fountain which never ceases to flow, and which still supplies the Abbey most plentifully with water."—(Annals.)

In the year 1740, several leaden pipes, running under ancient walls, were dug up, undoubtedly the work of brother Simon.

The following account of the Lavatory of S. Cuthbert's Monastery, Durham, may perhaps throw some light on the nature of the Lavatory at Waverley, and especially as they occupied similar situations :—

" The Lavatory, whose basin still remains in the middle of the cloister garth, was an octagon, having a door towards the refectory, and seven windows.  The monks could stand within it all round the basin, which had twenty-four brass taps, and the time for using it was at eleven a.m., before going into the refectory.  It was roofed over, and a dovecote was formed above the roof."—(Brit. Arch. Assoc. Rep., vol. xxii. 236.)

When Aubrey visited Waverley in 1673, (i. e.) about two hundred years ago, the Abbey was in a much more perfect condition than it is now.  He says—" Here is a fine rivulet, which runs under the house* and fences one side, but all the rest is walled.  By the lane are stately rocks of sand.  Within the walls are sixty

---

* Observe this arrangement—it was for drainage.  No doubt the discovery of the ancient culvert, about a century ago, gave rise to the story of a subterranean passage having been discovered at Waverley.

acres. The walls are very strong, and are chiefly of rag-stones ten foot high. Here remain walls of a fair Church, the walls of the cloister, and some part of the cloisters themselves, within the quadrangle of which hath been a pond (undoubtedly the Lavatory) then a marsh. There was also a chapel, larger than that of Trinity College, Oxford; the windows of the same fashion as the chapel windows of the priory of S. Mary in Wilts. There were no escutcheons or monuments remaining, but in the parlour and chamber over it, built not long since, were some roundels of painted glass, about eight inches diameter, viz.—S. Michael fighting with the devil; S. Dunstan holding the devil by the nose with his pincers, and having retorts, crucibles, and chemical instruments about him; with several others so exactly drawn as if done from a good modern print. The hall was very spacious and noble, with a row of pillars in the middle, and vaulted overhead. The very long building, with long narrow windows, in all probability, was the dormitory."—(Aubrey's Surrey, III, 160.)

What havoc has been made of the place in two hundred years! It is not silent decay, nor mere neglect which has done the mischief. The Abbey has been a quarry of squared stones, and hewn stones for the neighbourhood.* Hardly an ashler remains in its place.

* The long wall between the mill and the new school-room, at least (if not the mill itself) has been constructed of material from the ruins, for in this wall is a large stone with early Gothic mouldings, as if a portion of a window jamb, a column, or something of the kind.

The walls have been peeled like an orange, until nothing but the very rubble remains.

The celebrated Pugin was deeply moved when he saw the devastations committed on this ancient sanctuary, and no wonder.*

Much of the monastic pile has been altogether swept away; there is not the slightest trace of the Gateway, with its Chapel of S. Mary, the Infirmary of the Seculars, nor of the Chapel attached to the Infirmary, all of which are mentioned in the Annals.

---

# The Gateway and Bridges.

"ANNO 1223. A certain little boy, about seven or eight years of age, living at the gateway of Waverley, fell in the water, close to the gateway, on the day of the Invention of the Holy Cross, whom in a short time the current seized and, direct as an arrow, carried him beneath the four stone bridges; floating, therefore, upon the water, he was seen by some one, and taken from the stream, and the little which he had swallowed, he vomited. The day following, God being merciful, he was restored to his former

* "Thy servants think upon her stones, and it pitieth them to see her in the dust."

health, and he may be seen at this day, going in and out at the
gate, as heretofore."

There was also a

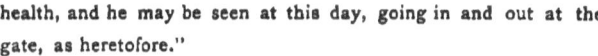

## Chapel at the Convent Gate,

dedicated to S. Mary; for Nicholas de Hely made provision for a
mass to be said annually, either here or in the great Church, with
other masses, for the benefit of his soul.—(See page 39.)

## The Infirmary of the Seculars.

"ANNO 1229. Adam, formerly Lord Abbot of Waverley, a
man commendable in religion, life, and doctrine, died this
year. He appointed that a private mass should be said
for each single lodger dying in the Infirmary of the Seculars on the
day, or the morrow, of their burial, for this custom was not observed in our house previously."—(Annals.)

Besides this Infirmary, the monks had one for themselves, with
which a Chapel was connected, and this was so arranged that the
sick lying on their beds might hear and join in the divine offices.

"Anno 1201. The Chapel of the Infirmary was dedicated on the

8th of the Ides of November, by Albino, Lord Bishop of Fernes in
Ireland, a monk of the Cistercian Order."—(Annals.)

This Chapel occurs again in 1263 :—" To be remembered by the
present, and laid up in store for future generations, is the record of
the pious memory of Matilda of London, the ' mother,' in a certain
degree of the monks of Waverley, buried in the Chapel of their Infirmary, on the 3rd of the Ides of February, in the year 1263.
Almost all her goods, as well in life as in death, she gave to
Waverley. Also, she provided for one lamp to be burning every
night in the Chapel of the said Infirmary, (the bell to be struck for
vigils, and the lamp thereupon to be lighted,) until after the celebra-
tion of masses in the Chapel in winter; and the light to be main-
tained in summer-time until after lauds; which same lamp, at
certain times, ought thus to burn, viz.—during all celebrations of
mass in the Chapel, and in the principal solemnities to both vespers
when three lamps are burnt in the choir."—(Annals.)

# Endowments and Benefactions.

ILLIAM Giffard, Bishop of Winchester, founder of the Convent, by his original charter, besides the land at Waverley,
with all its appurtenances in meadow and pasture, granted
to the monks two acres of land at Helestede, (Elstead) pannage for

their swine, with liberty to cut wood for fuel, and other necessary uses, in his coppices at Farnham.  This was in the year 1128.

Henry de Blois, brother of King Stephen, and Giffard's successor in the See of Winchester, added to this, of his own free gift, one virgate of land, lying at or near Waneford: also right of pasture for swine and other cattle at Farnham, in all such places as the free tenants, and others of the hundred, were wont to enjoy the same: with license to cut and dig heath, stone, sand, and all other earth whatsoever for their necessary uses, without let or hindrance.  This was about the year 1150.

In this charter of Henry de Blois, the bounds of their possessions, as they then stood, are described as follows :—" From the oak at Tileford, called ' Kynghoc,' along the king's highway to Farnham, as far as Winterbourn (some water-course probably dry in summer) and from thence along the bank which runs from Farnham, to the hill called Richard's Hulle, (some suppose Crooksbury) and across the said hill and the bridge of Waneford to the meadow of Tileford, called ' Ilvethammes-mede,' and so to the oak from whence this perambulation sets out."

Other benefactions were—

1.—Adeliza, second queen of Henry I, who died 1151.  She gave to the Convent the Grange of Northolt, with the woods thereto belonging.  Her second husband was William de Albini, Earl of Arundel, who died at Waverley Abbey in 1176.

2.—King Stephen gave them Netham, near Alton, and the Church of Farnham, and his gift was confirmed to them by Henry III in 1239. (Part of the Netham estate was purchased by the monks about 1245.)

3.—Bochild was added to their estates by Alan, son of Pagan de Villers.

4.—Wanborough, near Puttenham, was given them for 120 marks of silver, by Pharamuse de Bologne, nephew of King Stephen's queen. It came to Waverley as early as the time of Gilbert, the second Abbot.

(From the large sum of money laid down by the Convent for this estate, it must have been a bona fide purchase, and cannot be regarded as a gift or endowment.)

" In the year 1279, William de Abbecroft gave and granted, and by his charter confirmed, to the monks of Waverley all his land of Abbecroft, which of them he held in chief, with the chief messuage and other of his appurtenances in Wanborough."*—(Annals.)

5.—Richer de Aquila, Lord of Witley, presented to the Convent the estate called Oxeneford, now a part of the Peper-Harow estate, on which a late Lord Middleton erected a gateway, intending it for an entrance to his park. Pugin was employed to furnish the design.

* This transaction is much like that of a copyholder presenting his copyhold to the Lord of the Manor.

6.—Ralph Picot, Sheriff of Surrey, added "Riehull," in Peper-Harow, about the year 1158.

7.—Cuserugge was presented by one Sewall de.........

8.—Richarde de Sifrewast gave the monks half a hide of land at Polementon, (perhaps Polehampton,) near Overton, Hants.

Among other donors were—

HUGO PEREGRINUS (the Palmer.)   The monks received him into the Abbey, and granted him food and clothing as one of the brethren; and on his death it was stipulated that he should be interred with all the obsequies of a monk.   To Nichola, his wife, they gave two marks of silver, and she confirmed the grant.   The witnesses were Richard de Manerio, and Robert his son.

This Hugh Peregrinus is simply Hugh "Manory."

Richard de Manerio, who is also termed Richard Peregrinus, of Ash, gave a parcel of woodland to the Convent, which gift was confirmed by his son Robert, and by John, the son of Robert.   This grant of Robert Manory, in the Bull of Pope Eugenius, is called the Grange of Nutshelf, in Hants.*

* Two brass memorials of the Manorys, with their shield of arms (a cross engrailled) still remain in Ash Church.

(1) "Of yor charite pray for the sovle of Thomas Manory, of whose sovle ihu have m'cy, which Thomas dyed the xx day of decembre, the yer' of o' Lord M.v<sup>c.</sup> & xvi." 1516)

(2) "Of yor charite, pray for the soul of Anne Vyne, daughter and heire of Thomas Manory, on whose soule ihu have m'cy."

The Manorys appear to have resided in the manor of Cleygate, in Ash, recently purchased by Capt. Mangles.

A tenement and land, called *Frymlesworth,* is described in an ancient document,

Amongst other possessions of Waverley, were Duckenfield, Wis-
hanger, Bomata Grange, Serveton Grange, Dumnore Grange, Laga
Grange, Tongham Grange, a hide in Ebbesburn.

In the time of King John, Gilbert de Basseville gave them a place
in Worplesdon, which the monks termed the "New Rude."—(Annals)

In 1260, Hugh de Polsted gave the monks in Frank Almoign his
wood in Compton, called "Inwood," with liberty to enclose it.

In 1263, Maud of London, termed "Mother to the Convent,"
gave them, by will, one hundred marks, to be laid out in lands, out of
the proceeds of which two pittances were to be given to the monks;

probably written tem Eliz., as having been held, first by Stephen Manory, next by
Thomas Manory, and then by John, who paid a quit-rent of 8s. 4d. per annum. This
John was living in 1566.

Thomas, another of the family, held, by copy, dated 1542, a piece of ground in
Ffrymlesworth, and another piece called "Youngs."

There are three entries of them in Ash Register. "Jone, bap. 1551; Thomas, in
1554; and George the son of George, in 1602," which appears to have been the last.

In 1656, John Styles lived in a house at Ash, "heretofore Robert Mannerings."—
Ch. Reg.

A Robert Manory resided within the Manor of Wanborough, in 1584.

A branch of this family was settled at Puttenham at an early period.

In the reign of Ed. I, *Cutt Mill*, in Puttenham, was given by John de Cotte, or
Cutte, to John *le Paumer*, (Peregrinus) as the marriage portion of his daughter,
Juliana de Cotte. In 1466, the mill was again in the hands of *John Manory*. Two
hundred years ago there were a brass of the Manorys in Puttenham Church, which is
thus described by Aubrey:—

"On a scroll of brass issuing from the mouth of a woman."

"O Mater Dei memento mei;" and underneath, on a plate of brass, "Orate pro aia
Agnet' Manory, vidue que obiit iij dia Junii ano dni Mil. cccc. lxxxij. cui' aie ppcietur
Deus. Amen. (This brass is not in existence.)

There are ten entries of them in the oldest register of Puttenham, the latest of
which is dated 1602; and there was a tenement in the village which went by the
name of "*Manories*," as late as 1690. In *Seale* register is a record of the baptism of
Margaret dau. of Arnald Manner, in 1540.

one on her obit, and the other on the 13th of December, being the
obit of her husband; Lebert. With the money was purchased a
tenement in Surweton, of Richard de Totteford, clerk, and 29s. 6d.
per annum was reserved out of the rent of it for the two pittances.
Accordingly, a portion of bread and fish was dealt to each monk on
the 6th of the Ides of February annually, on which day the donor
died, and another of fish on the feast of S. Lucy, being the obit of
her husband.—(Annals.)

Other provision for lights to be burnt in the Infirmary Chapel
has already been mentioned.

Nicholas de Hely, Bishop of Winchester, died in 1279; but it was
not until 1310 that any provision was made for his soul's welfare at
Waverley. Then, however, Hugo Tripacy, parson of Martin Worthy,
near Winchester, had license to grant to the Convent of Waverley
the manor of Cuserugge, with a messuage and fifty-nine acres of
land, five of pasture and four of wood, in Chivele, for the main-
tenance of a chaplain in the conventual Church at Waverley, to pray
for the soul of Nicholas, late Bishop of Winchester. This manor
of Cuserugge was to be held of the Abbot of D'Aumone (mother
Abbey of Waverley) by the service of one clove gillyflower, and the
messuage and land of the Abbot of Abingdon, at 5s. per annum.

On 25th July the same year, it was covenanted by the Convent, in
consideration of this endowment,—

1st.—To celebrate mass annually in the Chapel of S. Mary at the gate of their Convent, or in the Abbey Church, for the soul of Nicholas de Hely, who dedicated the Church of Waverley, and was there interred. Also one mass weekly by one of the brethren of the house, and one other daily by the precentor or succentor.

2nd.—To celebrate his obit on the 12th of February yearly, that being the day of his death.

3rd.—To distribute annually among the monks on the same day, spicery, as a remuneration for their trouble, to the value of five marks, in equal portions.

4th.—Another mark (13s. 4d.) was to be spent in additional viands on that day for the Refectory table.

5th.—On the same day new shoes to the value of twenty shillings, were to be distributed by the porter to poor widows at the Abbey gate. The prior cellarer to receive the same sum from the manor of Cuserugge yearly for this purpose, on S. John Baptist's day.

6th.—They also engaged to provide a wax taper to be set in a brass candlestick at the head of the said Bishop's grave, to burn there on his anniversary, and on other solemn days, at high mass.

7th.—To maintain and keep up a cross of marble, set up by the executors of the Bishop at Froyle, and in case it be broken or thrown down by lightning, thunder, or other storm, to erect another in its place.

8th.—To remember the said master, Hugh Tripacy, in all their masses, as well during his life as after his decease.

Their liberties in Wanborough and Bramley were confirmed to them by Edward III.

Anno 5 Edward II, (1312). By a charter of this date, the Convent received a patent for receiving a pipe of red wine annually out of the port of Southampton (which said grant was renewed in 2 Edward IV., where it is expressly said to have been given them for the consecration of the Body and Blood of Jesus Christ in the Blessed Sacrament.

Anno 1363. John de Netherhaven gave a messuage and eighty acres of land—two of meadow, sixteen of moorland, three of heath, rents amounting to 30s. 4d. in Farnham, and one pound of pepper— to celebrate an anniversary for his soul, the same being held of the Bishop of Winchester, as of his castle of Farnham, by a rent of 21s. per annum, suit of court to manor of Farnham, and keeping in repair thirty feet of the park enclosure there. The value of this estate to the Convent amounted to £4 0s. 6d. per annum.

The Abbey lands, when first given to the Convent, were, for the most part, wild and uncultivated, and the brethren had the task of clearing and rendering the ground serviceable—no very light or easy undertaking, e. g. :—

In 1248, the Abbot obtained permission to clear nine acres of ground at Beecham, in the forest of Alice Holt. Probably this was parcel of the thirty-five acres of land granted by Henry III. to the Abbot of Waverley, in the year 1239. —(Rot. Pat. 23. xx, iii. Ro. 5.)

In 1309, the Abbot was permitted to clear and enclose forty acres of woodland at Dockenesfield, within the bounds of the forest of Wolvermere or Woolmer.—(Cal. Rot. Pat.)

In 1315, the Abbot paid twenty shillings to the king for license to enclose forty acres of his wood at Drokenesfeld, within the bounds of the king's forest of Wolvermere.—(Abb. Treasury Rolls. 8 Ed. II. Ro. 10.)

In 1333, the Abbot paid a mark into the royal treasury for license to clear forty acres of his wood at Dokenfeld, in the forest of Wolmere, and to bring the land into cultivation.—(Treasury Roll, 6 Ed. III. Extract Reddis. Ro. 35.)

---

# The Rental of Waverley,

as it was attested by William Ayling, the last Abbot in 1536. The original document is in the Record Office.

" THE site of the monastery of the Blessed Mary, the Virgin of Waverley, including the ......... and divers houses, with the garden and the little garden, situated within the Abbey precincts there, was estimated to be worth xls.

" The Abbey Farm or demesne, in the hands of the Abbot, consisting of divers parcels of arable, meadow, and pasture land, pertaining to the office of Cook of the Monastery, as by the oath of William Ayling, Abbot of the monastery there, as by other declarations of his, made in the presence of Richard Weston and divers other commissioners, was valued at £14 14s. 1od."

" The assize rents, with other returns from divers villages, hamlets, and parishes, were as follow—

|  | £ | s. | d. |
|---|---|---|---|
| WANBOROUGH .. .. .. .. | 35 | 8 | 6 |
| HOOGSHOT (Stoke D'Abernon).. | 4 | 0 | 0 |
| TONGHAM .. .. .. .. .. | 2 | 13 | 4 |
| (This estate comprised 100 acres.) | | | |
| OFORD .. .. .. .. .. .. | 4 | 13 | 4 |
| PEPER-HAROWE .. .. .. | 1 | 6 | 8 |
| MERWIKE .. .. .. .. .. | 1 | 19 | 6 " |
| (In neighbourhood of Hambledon.) | | | |

" The MILLS produced as follows—

|  | £ | s. | d. |  |
|---|---|---|---|---|
| OWT MYLL .. .. .. .. .. | 4 | 0 | 0 | ⎫ |
| WANFORD MYLL .. .. .. | 2 | 10 | 0 | ⎬ £10 10 0 |
| WADON MYLL .. .. .. .. | 4 | 0 | 0" | ⎭ |

WOODS at Wanborough produced 13s 4d. per annum.

The POND at Wanborough produced 6s. 8d. per annum.

(There are traces of a very large pond below the mill. The deep mill flash has been cut through it in more recent times.)

The sale of the perquisites of courts and other fines were—

| Of WANBOROUGH .. .. .. .. | 3s. 4d. |
|---|---|
| Of MARKWIKE .. .. .. .. | 4s. 0d. |

The yearly offerings and oblations made by pilgrims and other

persons in the Chapel of S. Bartholomew, Wanborough, amounted
to 13s. 4d.

The various rents of their other estates were as follows—

|  | £ | s. | d. |
|---|---|---|---|
| DOKKINFELD .. .. .. .. | 40 | 2 | 0 |
| NETHAM .. .. .. .. .. | 55 | 16 | 6 |
| BOVYATE .. .. .. .. .. | 18 | 18 | 0 |
| SWARNETON .. .. .. .. | 6 | 6 | 8 (? Serveton) |
| NUTSHAWE .. .. .. .. .. | 4 | 8 | 4 |
| DUNMERE .. .. .. .. .. | 0 | 5 | 0 |

The Woods at Neatham were worth 3s. 4d. per annum.

Perquisites of courts were—

| Of DOKKEYNFELD .. .. .. | 4s. 0d. |
|---|---|
| NEATHAM.. .. .. .. .. | 6s. 8d. |
| BOVAT .. .. .. .. .. | 6s. 8d. |

Rent of manor farm of Shawe, 106s. 8d.

Rent of property in London, 20s. per annum.

Assize and other rents in—

|  | £ | s. | d. |
|---|---|---|---|
| ROGATE... ... ... ... ... ... | 8 | 13 | 4 |
| NORTHOLTE ... ... ... ... | 4 | 0 | 0 |
| YAPTON... ... ... ... ... ... | 0 | 16 | 0 |
| CHICHESTER ... ... ... ... | 0 | 8 | 4 |

The farmer of the manor of Berford paid 12s., and of Criwe-
chester, 20s.

Total income...........£197 13s. 10½d.

This was not all clear profit, however, some of it had to be disbursed :—

| | | | |
|---|---|---|---|
| On OXTED was charged | ... ... | 26s. 8d. | |
| MERKWIKE | ... ... ... ... | 10s. 7d. | £4 16 7 |
| TONGHAM... | ... ... ... | 6s. 0d. | |
| MILL OF WATON ... | ... ... | 53s. 4d. | |

The stipend of the bailiff of Wanborough was 20s., and the bailiff of Merkwike, 5s.

The stipend of William Lussher,* chief steward of the monastery, was £2 13s. 4d. per annum.

Richard Mathew, auditor received 20s.

The Prioress of Dartford received 12s. yearly for pannage of pigs.

Five shillings were paid to the Archdeacon of Surrey for procurations and synodals for the Chapel of Wanborough.

There was yearly distributed to the poor, the sum of £4 10s. 0d. by obligation.

The king's bailiff of Alton was paid 12s. 4d. for certain lands in Neatham. The Abbot of Rodying received 53s. 4d. for lands in Bovyat.

The bailiff of Netham received 20s., and the bailiff of Dokkenfield 13s. 4d.

There was paid 46s. 8d. to the Abbot of Hyde for the pannage of pigs out of the monastic bounds at Netham.

The Rector of Dunmere also received 40s.

And all these payments were estimated at £22 5s. 8d., so that the clear income of the Abbey was £174 8s. 3½d.

* The Lusshers were of Shoelands House in Puttenham.

# Abbots of Waverley.

OHN, the first Abbot, was one of the twelve who came from D'Aumone in the year 1128. He died the same year, and was succeeded by

GILBERT, who was present at the translation of the body of S. Erkenwold in S. Paul's, London. Gilbert is mentioned in a document, dated 1145, preserved in the Memorial House at Winchester.

HENRY, the third Abbot, died 1182, and was succeeded by*

HENRY DE CIRENCESTER, a monk of Waverley, who resigned in 1187, and was succeeded by

CHRISTOPHER, formerly Abbot of Brewern, fifth Abbot. In his time there were in the house 120 lay brethren and seventy monks, and they had thirty caracutes of ploughland, i. e. thirty teams of oxen at work. In his time the Convent gave one year's stock of their wool towards the ransom of Richard I., taken prisoner by the Emperor of Austria. In 1196, this Abbot was removed, and was succeeded by

JOHN, the hospitaller, a monk of Waverley, who died at Merton, the 16th of September, (16 Kal. Oct.) 1201.

* Winchester documents.

JOHN, the cellarer,* was elected Abbot in his stead. He died in 1216.

ADAM I., Sub-Prior of Waverley, was next appointed. He resigned in 1219. By his counsel and aid the great bell was provided the year before."—(Annals.)

ADAM II., the eighth Abbot, formerly Abbot of Gerondon† Leicesters, succeeded to the abbacy. In his time, " Anno 1221, the

---

* The cellarer's office was one of great responsibility. He was entrusted with the general management of the affairs of the society. He had the care of every thing relating to the food of the monks as well as of the *cellar*, kitchen, and refectory. Some of his duties were prescribed with singular minuteness, (*e. g.*) he was to collect the spoons after dinner, and in so doing he was to carry the Abbot's in his right hand, and the rest in his left.

The cellarer of S. Albans, Herts, had the supervision and management of the courts leet and baron held under the Abbot.

The office was not a permanent one, but the more competent of the monks held it as they were elected yearly.

[Mrs. Howard, of Greystoke and Thornbury, has the original transcripts on parchment of the Court Rolls of Barnet and Chipping-Barnet, *made by the monks of S. Albans, Herts, for the use of their cellarers.* They form two immense folios, most beautifully written, commencing 30 Hen. III, (1246) and continued to the commencement of the seventeenth century by subsequent owners.]

† The following abbeys were offshoots from Waverley :—

GERONDON Leicesters, founded in 1132 (5 Kal. Nov.) by Robert, Earl of Leicester. Its chartulary is preserved in the British Museum. (Lansd. MS. 415.)

FORD, in Devon, founded 5 nones May, 1135, (Annals.)

BRIGHTLEY, Devon, founded 1136, afterwards removed to Ford.

TAME, or Thame, (Oxfords) founded 1138, removed from Ottley. Extracts from its chartulary may be found Brit. Mus. Cott. MS. Jul. c. vii, and in Bodl. Lib. Dodesworth MS. vol. 141. Also *Fragmenta* at Christ's Ch. Coll., Oxford.

COMBE, (Warwick) founded 1150. Its chartulary is in the British Museum, Cott. MS. Vitell. A. i, and D. xvii.

Possibly there may be more information about Waverley in these chartularies. The writer regrets that he has not had time to consult them.

seal of our house was changed* on the morrow of the Blessed
Calixtus, Pope and Martyr."—(Annals.)  He resigned in 1234.

WALTER GIFFARD, formerly Abbot of Bettlesdon, was elected
in his stead.  This was the Abbot who bestirred himself so strenu-
ously in defence of the privileges of the Abbey, when its right of
sanctuary was infringed in the case of the homicide—(see miscellaneous Extracts from the Annals.)  He was evidently a man of con-
siderable weight; since we find Isabella, Countess of Arundel, when
wishing to found a Cistercian Abbey for nuns at Marham, con-
sulting him, and obtaining permission to enter the Convent at
Waverley for this purpose from the Pope himself.

The estate of Graffham, in Dunsfold, was granted by this Abbot
about the year 1238, to Walter de Grapham.  He was succeeded by

RALPH, Abbot of Dunkesweel (Donkville Co-Devon) and previously Abbot of Tintern.  He was highly distinguished for his in-

---

* There is an impression of this new seal in the British Museum, a sulphur cast of
which is in the possession of Mr Nealds, of Guildford.  It has the usual form of the
"Vesica Piscis," and bears, under a handsome canopy, a figure of the Blessed Virgin
enthroned, with the Holy Child on her left arm.  In her right hand, resting on the
throne, is a stem of lilies.  Beneath her feet, under an arch, is a kneeling figure
in the attitude of devotion.  The legend, in Lombardic capitals, is almost defaced.  The
following only is legible :—" ....ATIS ET CONV....  ....E WAVER...."
Two other seals are engraved in Brayley's History of Surrey.  One, an oval,
has a Lombardic A, with the head of a pastoral staff rising from the top of
the letter.  The other, somewhat larger, and of the usual pointed form, has a right
hand grasping a pastoral staff, the head of which is turned *towards* the bearer,
to indicate his internal and *domestic rule*.  (A Bishop's staff has the crook reversed,
to indicate his outward and diocesan care.)  This seal has the following marginal
inscription :—" COM : SIGL : ABBACIE : WAVERLEIA."

tegrity and knowledge, and resigned his rule in the year 1266, because of his failing health, owing to his arduous labours. His notary,

WILLIAM OF LONDON, a monk of Waverley, succeeded to the abbacy. The next Abbot,

WILLIAM DE HUNGERFORD, resigned in the year 1276. " So paralyzed was he that he could not superintend the affairs and estate of the Convent any longer."—(Annals)  To him succeeded

HUGO OF LEWKNOR, a monk of Waverley. He was elected canonically by the Convent on the feast of S. Edmund, Archbishop, and was installed by John, then Abbot of Tintern. He died in 1285, when

PHILIP DE BEDEWIND, a monk of Waverley, was elected in his stead; and on Easter-day following he received episcopal benediction in the cathedral Church of Winchester."—(Annals.)

(The following Abbots are from the History of Surrey, by Manning and Bray.)

WILLIAM occurs in 1312. (Query.—Was this the Abbot of Waverley who was present at the Parliament held at Carlisle in 1307 ?)

ROBERT, mentioned in a MS. of 1335.

JOHN, living in 1344.

WILLIAM HAKELSTONE, Abbot of Waverley, died in 1399, when

JOHN BOYD was elected by the Convent.

WILLIAM occurs 1452.

WILLIAM MARTYN, a monk of Waverley, elected Abbot, 1456.

THOMAS, (? Skevington) appointed Bishop of Bangor in 1509.

WILLIAM occurs in Bishop Fox's Register in 1511 and 1522.

JOHN, Abbot of Waverley, occurs in 1529.

(So far Manning and Bray.)

WILLIAM ALYNG, the last Abbot of Waverley, surrendered the Abbey and its estates to the King's Commissioner in 1536, when he attested to the correctness of the returns relating to the revenues of the Convent.—(See ' Rental.')

## Extracts from the Annals of Waverley. (Translations)

ANNO 1128. " This year the Abbey of Waverley was founded by William Giffard, Lord Bishop of Winchester, viij Kal. December.  And he (Bishop William) died the same year, and Henry of Blois, the brother of King Stephen succeeded, who was Abbot of Glastonbury.  And John, the first Abbot of Waverley, who came with the Convent, died this year at Midehurst, returning from a chapter."

Anno 1180.  " William, Abbot of Kingswood, was deposed, and Eudo, Prior of Waverley, succeeded."

Anno 1201. " There was a great flood at Waverley, by which the Abbey was almost submerged, and greatly imperilled."

Anno 1217. " This year, Aalis de Salerne, of excellent memory, a nun of Puttenham, and a woman of austere life, died. She was a lover of every virtue."

Anno 1218. " Richard, formerly Prior of Waverley, was made Abbot of Bruern."

Anno 1232. (A question arose as the seniority of the Abbeys of Waverley and Furness. It was settled in favour of Waverley.)

Anno 1233, 5 Ides July, (July 11th.) " A terrible tempest, most vehemently raging, arose in the house of Waverley, destroying the stone bridges, and beating down the walls, the water impetuously sweeping through the cloister and all the offices, and even prevailing as far as the new monastery, in many places attaining the height of eight feet."—(See also under ' Treasury.')

Anno 1240. (There is a long account in the Annals of ' Violation of Sanctuary ' this year. The following excellent summary of the affair is taken from the ' Preface ' to the Annals. It should be understood that Waverley had the privilege of ' Sanctuary.') :—

" A young shoemaker came to the Abbey at Easter time, and was employed in his art within its precincts. There had been a charge of homicide against him, and some three or four months afterwards the officers sent to apprehend him, seized him there, and in spite of the anathema of the Abbot and the protests of the seniors of the

monastery, who declared their precincts to be privileged (even as
the altars of Churches) he was bound and carried off to prison. The
excitement in the Abbey was immense, the privileges of the whole
Order (as the chronicler observes) were in danger. If men could be
thus bound in their Abbeys or Granges, there would in future be no
distinction between the houses of the religious and those of the
seculars. The services, even the solemn masses, were stopped. The
Abbot went at once to the legate (Otho) who is described as only
dissimulating and idling about the matter, He then went to the King
himself, and with sighs and tears brought his complaint, insisting
that the King could only satisfy God and the Order, but by causing
the man (so violently removed) to be restored to the holy place.
The King is described as at once giving way, and granting the
Abbot's request ; but the council opposed, and a day was appointed
for discussing the privileges of the Order. The King himself seems
to have interfered to stop the suspension of the services, and on
August 10th (the man had been carried off on the 8th) they were
resumed. The council opposed the privileges strongly, 'most per-
versely interpreting the apostolical writings, and expounding them
maliciously,' and gave their answer against the Order; whence
(says the chronicler) it cannot easily be understood or explained
with what grief of heart, with what bitterness of soul, the Abbot opposed himself for the defence of his liberties. At last, however, the
privileges were proved to the King and council in such a way as to

make it clear that the Abbey precincts did possess, by the Pope's authority, the right that were claimed for them, and that all violators of them, and of those who consented to their violation, were excommunicate. The man was then at once, by the King's order, brought back by the same officers to the Abbey, to the joy of the neighbourhord, and the officers were excommunicated, and only restored after satisfaction had been done to God and the Abbey, and they had been publickly scourged by the Dean of that place (Prior) and the Vicar of Farnham. They became in future (says the chronicler) more respectful to our Order."

Anno 1229. "Adam, formerly Abbot of Waverley, a man commendable in religion, life, and doctrine, died this year. He appointed that a private mass should be said for each lodger dying in the Infirmary of the Seculars, either on the day or morrow of their burial, which was not done in our house previously."

Anno 1239. "This year the Church of Frensham was removed from the place where it was first situated to another place, by the advice and assistance of Luke, Archdeacon at Surrey, and was dedicated this same year."

Anno 1245. "Litera Dominicalis B. dies Paschæ, xvi. Kal. Maii. Eodem anno, dominus Radulphus, monachus Sanctæ Mariæ de Waverleia, qui quondam abbatizaverit in domo de Tinterna, electus est in abbatem de Donekweel: vir quidem morum gravitate ac sapientiæ fulgore non mediocriter adornatus."

Anno 1250. "William de Ralegar, Bishop of Winchester, died in France. Before he left England he gave and confirmed to us by his charter, a site for a fish-pond on his heath within his warren of Farnham; which site begins from the little bridge beyond Tilford, extending itself by the watercourse, which is called Crikeledeburne, unto Cherte; paying yearly for the aforesaid fishery, to him or his successors, the sum of half a mark. In this year the fish-pond was commenced, but is not yet finished."*

Anno 1250. "By permission of William de Raleger, Lord Bishop of Winchester, and of Peter de Ryeval, rector of the church of Alton, it was granted to us this year to celebrate divine service in the oratory, which is within the bounds of our Grange at Netham, all right and authority belonging to the Bishop of Winchester, together with an indemnity to the mother church of Alton and the chapel of Haliburn being reserved; i. e. in this manner—That we there celebrate without beating of bells and distribution of sacraments to our brethren. That we do not receive the confessions of secular persons there except at the point of death, but that all our domestics and servants at the Grange, resort to the chapel of Haliburn for hearing divine service, and for receiving the sacraments

---

* "*Abbot's Pond*" occupied an area of about fourteen acres. "An eruption of the pond-head, causing much havoc and devastation, took place Nov. 29, 1841, at a time when the pond had been penned about eighteen inches higher than ever before. The stone-work of the pen-stock and three hundred cubic yards of earth, forming the embankment, were entirely borne down. The pond has since been drained, and the land cultivated."—(*Brayley's Surrey.*)

of the church, and that they remain subject to the same, as here-tofore."

Anno 1262. " This year died William Abbot of Combe, formerly monk of Waverley. William, Abbot of Ford, died at Waverley, and was buried there in the Chapter-house."

Anno 1277. " This year there prevailed throughout all the region of England, a general scab of sheep, which, by the common people, is called 'Clausic,' (? Claw-sick, a foot disease) by which all the sheep of the land are infected ; for the removal of which disease, (scabiem) there has been discovered a certain ointment, made of quicksilver and hog's lard."

Anno 1279. "Jordanus de Twangham (Tongham) then Prior of Waverley, made Abbot of Combe in Devon, in the place of Warinus, who resigned."

Anno 1283. (There was a dispute between Peter de Sancto Mario, Archdeacon of Surrey and the Convent of Waverley, concerning the payment of small tithes. The controversy was terminated by the Bishop, who was appointed arbitor.)

Anno 1188. " Such an abundant harvest, that a quarter of corn (frumenti) was sold for two shillings."

# The Dissolution.

WILLIAM Ayling, the last Abbot of Waverley, surrendered the Conventual Estate into the hands of Richard Weston and divers other Commissioners, in the year 1536.*

# A few Particulars

## connected with the breaking up of Monastic Institutions,

### CHIEFLY GATHERED FROM JOHN STOW'S ANNALS.

"THE religious persons that were in the said houses were cleerely put out: some went to the other greater houses: some went abroad to the world. It was (saith mine author) a pitiful thing to hear the lamentation that the people in the country made for them ; for there was great hospitalitie kept among them ; and so it was thought more than 10,000 persons—masters and servants had lost their livings by the putting downe of the lesser houses at that time."—(Stow.)

* Record Office—Miscellaneous Books, No. 406.

1535, October. "The King sent Master Thomas Cromwell, and Dr. Lee, and others, to visite the Abbeys, Priories and Nunneries in England......... They took out of monasteries and abbes their relickes and chiefest jewels to the Kinge's use, they said."

(The following extract shews the fate of a portion of these religious spoils :—"Anno 1541. On Christmas even, at seaven of the clocke at night, beganne a great fire in the house, sometime named 'Elsing Spittle', then the house of Sir John Williams, master of the King's jewels, where many of these jewels were brent, and more embezled, as was thought."—Stow.)

The loss inflicted upon literature by the Dissolution of Religious Houses can hardly be estimated. Bishop Bale, in his ' Declaration,' has given us a melancholy view of the state of things that prevailed in consequence :—"A number of them which purchased these (religious houses) reserved of those library books, some to rub their jakes, some to scovr their candlesticks, some to rub their boots, and some they sold to the grocers and soap-sellers, and some they sent over sea to the bookbinders ; not in small numbers, but at times, whole ships full. I know a merchantman (which at this time shall be nameless) that bought the contents of two noble libraries for forty shillings apiece, a shame it is to be spoken. This stuff he hath occupied, instead of grey paper, by the space of more than these ten years, and yet hath he store enough for as many years to come."

" 1533.  Christ Church, London, was suppressed : Canons sent to other houses.  Their church plate and lands given to Sir Thomas Audley, late made keeper of the great seal."—(Stow.)

# Sufferings of Monastics.

MARCH 10, 1537, John Paslew, B.D., Abbot of Whalley, Lincolns, executed at Lancaster.  About 13th of March, the Abbot of Sawley, in Lancashire, was executed.

Robert Hops, Abbot of Woburn, Beds, and the Prior of his house, were put to death at Woburn.

March 29, A Lincolnshire Abbot was executed at Tyburn.

1538.  In the month of June, William Thursk, Abbot of Fountains, Adam Sodbury, Abbot of Gervaux, the Abbot of Rivaulx, Yorks, were put to death at Tyburn.

1539.  " In the moneth of November, Hugh Faringdon, Abbot of Reading, was hanged and quartered at Reading,  The same day, was Richard Whiting, Abbot of Glastonbury, hanged and quartered on Torre Hill, besides his monastery.  Also, shortly after, John Bech, Abbot of Colchester, was executed at Colchester, all for denying the King's supremacy."—(Stow.)

The Charter-house, London, was the home of the Chartreuse, or Carthusian monks, and hardly any religious fraternity at the Disso-lution bore such noble testimony to the evidence of conscience as they.

On the 29th April, 1535, John Houghton, its Prior, was hanged, drawn, and quartered at Tyburn, for denying the King's supremacy, and one of his quarters suspended on the Charter-house, as a warning to the brotherhood. This poor limb did its work. On the 18th of June following, three more monks of the Charter-house, viz.—Thomas Exmew, Humfrey Middlemore, (proctor) and Se-bastian Nidigate, were hanged and quartered on the scene of their prior's sufferings. For the same offence, on the 4th of August, 1540, William Horne, a lay brother of the same establishment, fol-lowed his companions through the same death struggle.

In what light these poor sufferers were regarded at the time, the following extract from Stow's Annals will shew :—"Anno 1547. The first of July two priests were arraigned and condemned in the Guildhall, for keeping of certaine reliques, amongst the which there was a lefte arme and shoulder of a monk, of the Charter-house, on the which arme was written, 'It was the arme of suche a monke which suffered martirdome under King Henry the Eighth."

There was another, named Rochester, whom Cranmer tried in vain to convert to royal supremacy. He was the sixth victim.

From first to last only six were drawn aside from their resolution, the rest were executed."—(See "Old England," vol. ii, p. 371.)

Of the fate of the Abbot and monks of Waverley, history is silent; but this much is certain, they were turned out homeless into the wide world, and their estates conferred upon a royal favourite.

---

On the 20th July, 1536, Sir William Fitz Williams, Knight of the Garter, and treasurer of the king's household, soon afterwards Earl of Southampton and privy seal, had a grant of the Abbey, with house, church, church-yard, messuages, and lands thereto belonging, the manors of Waverley, Wanborowe, Markweke, Monkenhoke in Surrey; the rectories of Waverley and Wanborowe in Surrey, and of Netham, Sawroton and Roviat in Hants: the manors of Dokynfeld in Surrey, and Shawe in Berks; all mills and advowsons in Waverley, Stoke D'Abernon, Dunsfold, Shallesford, Alford, Wytteley, Seale, Southwerk, Godalmyne, Wokyng, Worplesdon, Farnham, Elsteed, Puttenham, Peper Harowe, and Frynsham in Surrey. The reserved rent* for the whole being £23 12s. 10½d.

Sir William Fitz Williams died without issue, in 1543,† leaving Waverley to Sir Anthony Brown, his uterine brother, whose son, Anthony Brown, Viscount Montacute, died in 1592, leaving it to his

---

* In 1626, this rent, amounting to £17 8s. 10d., was granted by Charles I. to his Queen, Henrietta Maria.—Rymer's Fœdera, vol. viii. P. II. page 51.

† His relict, "Ladye Mabell Fitzwilliams come of Southampton," was buried at Farnham, Aug. 21, 1550.—Ch. Reg.

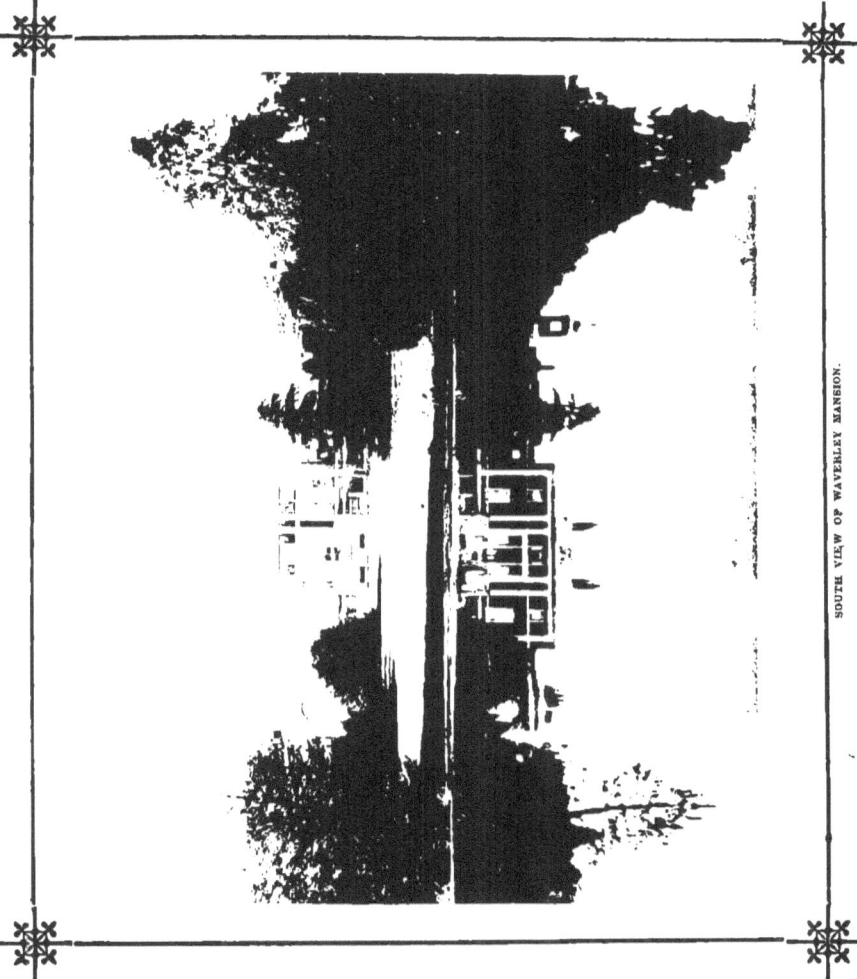

SOUTH VIEW OF WAVERLEY MANSION.

son, Anthony, who sold the Waverley Estate to the Coldham*
family, who eventually sold it to William Aislabie, Esq. The next
. owner was Mr. Child, an attorney at Guildford. His son, or
nephew, Charles, sold it again in 1747, to Thomas Orby Hunter,
Esq., who died in 1770. In the following year, this estate was con-
veyed by his son Charles to the trustees of Field-Marshal Sir Robert
Rich, Bart., then deceased. His son, Sir Robert Rich, died in 1786,
leaving a daughter and heiress, Mary Frances, who became the wife
of Rev. Charles Bostock, LLD., who took the name of Rich, and
was created a Baronet by George III. in 1792. About four years
afterwards, (Brayley) those parties disposed of Waverley to John
Thomson, Esq., who assumed the name of Poulett in 1820. Waverley became the property of George Thomas Nicholson, Esq.,
in 1830. About the year 1869, it was purchased by Thomas D.
Anderson, Esq., the present owner.

* It was during the time of the Coldhams that Waverley suffered most, according
to Dr. Agee, when it was reduced from an imposing, though ruined pile, to mere
heaps of shapeless rubble. But the work of demolition must have commenced at a
much earlier period, for the domestic papers preserved at Loseley Park contain
notices of " *wagon loads of rubbish* " brought from Waverley Abbey, for the con-
struction of that house, 1562-8.

FINIS.

ANDREWS AND SON, PRINTERS, GUILDFORD.

www.ingramcontent.com/pod-product-compliance
Lightning Source LLC
Chambersburg PA
CBHW032354020726
47499CB00008B/2748